A Balloon for Isabel

By *Deborah Underwood*   ILLUSTRATIONS BY *Laura Rankin*

 Greenwillow Books, *An Imprint of HarperCollins Publishers*

A Balloon for Isabel
Text copyright © 2010 by Deborah Underwood
Illustrations copyright © 2010 by Laura Rankin
All rights reserved. Manufactured in China.
For information address HarperCollins Children's Books,
a division of HarperCollins Publishers, 10 East 53rd Street, New York, NY 10022.
www.harpercollinschildrens.com

Gouache was used to prepare the full-color art.
The text type is Revival 555 BT.

Library of Congress Cataloging-in-Publication Data
Underwood, Deborah.
A balloon for Isabel / by Deborah Underwood ; illustrated by Laura Rankin.
p. cm.
"Greenwillow Books."
Summary: As graduation day approaches, Isabel tries to convince her teacher that
she and Walter, both porcupines, should receive balloons on the big day just like
the other children.
ISBN 978-0-06-177987-9 (trade bdg.)
[1. Porcupines—Fiction. 2. Balloons—Fiction. 3. Schools—Fiction.
4. Graduation (School)—Fiction. 5. Candy—Fiction.] I. Rankin, Laura, ill. II. Title.
PZ7.U4193Bal 2010   [E]—dc22   2009018759

10 11 12 13 14 SCP 10 9 8 7 6 5 4 3 2 1
First Edition

 Greenwillow Books

For Sophie,
with love—D. U.

For my friend C. V.,
who laughs in all the right places—L. R.

"No fair," said Isabel.

"Yeah, no fair," said Walter.

It was two days before graduation.

In two days the possums, the raccoons,
and all the other animals would get balloons.

But not the porcupines.

And Isabel wanted a balloon more than anything
in the whole world.

Ms. Quill smiled patiently. "I'm sorry, but balloons are not safe for porcupines. The porcupines will each get a lovely bookmark."

"But we already have Halloween bookmarks
and Valentine's bookmarks and—"

"And soon you will have lovely graduation
bookmarks," said Ms. Quill.

Isabel and Walter sat together at lunch.
"Can I have your broccoli?" asked Walter.
"I got jelly beans again."
"I wish *my* dad owned a candy shop,"
    said Isabel.

Isabel gazed out the window. "Sally told me that when you first get it, a balloon can bounce on the ceiling. If you pull the string and then let go, it makes a soft, thumpy sound," she said.

"I heard that after a few days, a balloon floats
halfway between the ceiling and the floor,"
said Walter. "It just hangs there like a ghost."

"Then it shrivels up so you can put it in your
empty olive jar with your other good stuff,"
said Isabel.

"A bookmark just sits there," said Walter.

"We *have* to get balloons," said Isabel. "I will
think of a plan."

The next day, during graduation song practice,
Isabel raised her paw.
"May the porcupines have balloons if we promise
to be very careful?" she asked.

Ms. Quill wrote something on the board. "Porcupines plus balloons equals . . ."

"Happiness?"
asked Isabel.

"Trouble," said Ms. Quill.
"If a balloon popped on your
quills, it would scare you."

"I am not scared of anything,
except the vacuum cleaner,"
said Isabel.

"Then it would
scare someone else."

Walter raised his paw.
"It would not scare me."

"A popped balloon could fly through
the air and hit someone in the eye,"
said Ms. Quill.

"We could wear goggles,"
said Isabel.

"That is enough," said
Ms. Quill. "I know you
would like balloons.
I would like one, too.
But the graduation bookmarks
are very nice this year."

"Was that your plan?" Walter asked Isabel.
"It was not my *only* plan," Isabel said.

The next morning Isabel wore her pop-stopper to breakfast. But she got stuck in the doorway.

At recess Isabel and Walter strapped
pillows onto each other. But their quills
poked the pillows to pieces.

At lunchtime Isabel wrapped Walter in
packing bubbles. But the other kids tried
to pop *him.*

"Only one more day," Walter said sadly,
as they picked up their graduation caps.
"I'll think of something," Isabel said.
But inside she was not so sure.

That evening Isabel went to Walter's for a cookout.

"You sure have a lot of candy," she said.

"I know," said Walter.

"If you ever got a balloon, what color would it be?"
asked Isabel.

"Green," said Walter. "Like broccoli."

"I would get red," said Isabel. "Like a red . . .
I have an idea!"

The next day, the door to Ms. Quill's classroom flew open.
"We're pop-proofed!" shouted Isabel. "*Now* may we have balloons?"

Ms. Quill blinked. She stared. She touched one of
Isabel's gumdrops with her paw.
"I don't see why not," she said, finally.
"Hooray!" said Isabel.
"Hooray!" said Walter and the other porcupines.

"Are there any gumdrops left?" whispered Ms. Quill.

No porcupine at graduation was happier than Isabel.

Except maybe one.